Dear Readers,

I've always been afraid of large bugs and spiders. So when my husband and I bought a cabin in the woods of Pennsylvania years ago, I was unhappy to discover that there were lots of six- and eight-legged creatures sleeping in the corners and sometimes creeping across the floor.

One night I nearly fainted when I lifted a blanket off the sofa, and saw the biggest spider I'd ever seen. It was nearly the size of a saucer! The spider heard my screams, jumped off the sofa, and vanished between the floorboards.

"We have to leave now and never come back," I told my husband.

"I don't think so," he said. (He didn't mind spiders at all.)

Well, if we weren't going to run away, I knew the only thing to do was to get over my fears. And the best way to do that was to learn more about what I was afraid of. So I went to the library and checked out a dozen books on bugs and spiders.

I'd planned to gather cold, scientific information. But in the process, a number of bug names jumped off the page at me—leafwing butterflies, emperor moths, deathwatch beetles. I started making a list of all the names I liked, and a world of mystery and fantasy opened up. At the center was a remarkable detective named Spider Kane, who, in my mind, is that same scary creature I saw sitting on my sofa long ago.

He now invites you into his world...

MARY POPE OSBORNE

Spider Kane and the
Mystery at Jumbo Nightcrawler's

A STEPPING STONE BOOK™

Random House New York

For Bubba, Natalie, and Baby Mike —M.P.O.

Originally published as a Borzoi Book by Alfred A. Knopf, Inc., in 1993.
First Stepping Stone edition: 1999

www.randomhouse.com/kids

Library of Congress Cataloging-in-Publication Data:
Osborne, Mary Pope.
Spider Kane and the mystery at Jumbo Nightcrawler's / by Mary Pope Osborne ;
cover illustration by Will Terry. p. cm.

Summary: Lieutenant Leon Leafwing and Detective Spider Kane investigate the
mysterious disappearance of Leon's mother and members of the Order of the MOTH.
ISBN 0-679-80856-6 (trade) — ISBN 0-679-90856-0 (lib. bdg.)
[1. Mystery and detective stories. 2. Insects—Fiction.] I. Terry, Will, ill. II. Title.
PZ7.081167Sn 1993 [Fic]—dc21 91-10983

I'm like a poor fly;
Spiderman, please let me go.
I'm like a poor fly;
Spiderman, please let me go.
You got me locked up in your house,
And I can't break down your door.
                    —Bessie Smith
                        "The Spiderman Blues"

CAST OF CHARACTERS
(in order of appearance)

LEON LEAFWING—An earnest young leafwing butterfly; a lieutenant in the Order of the MOTH

MIMI—A gossamer-winged butterfly; Leon's girlfriend; an actress and a lieutenant in the Order of the MOTH

THOMAS "THE HAWK" HAWKINS—The greatest living actor in the moth world; a lieutenant in the Order of the MOTH

LA MÈRE LEAFWING—Leon Leafwing's mother; formerly known as "Pupa"

WALTER DOGTICK—La Mère Leafwing's companion; a grubby but well-meaning old tick

SARATOGA D'BEE—Hostess and singer bee at Jumbo Nightcrawler's Supper Club on Waterfront Row

JUMBO NIGHTCRAWLER—Biggest worm on the waterfront; owner of a jazz supper club

JOHNNY ST. CLAIRE—Trumpet-playing housefly at Jumbo Nightcrawler's Supper Club

SPIDER KANE—Amateur sleuth; retired captain in the Mosquito Wars; jazz clarinetist; theater director; playwright; composer; leader of the Order of the MOTH; secret code name, "the Emperor Moth"

LITTLE PICKLES—Energetic, resourceful ladybug; a lieutenant in the Order of the MOTH; caterer and maker of tulip cradles

ROSIE—Little Pickles's partner; former lieutenant in the Mosquito Wars; member of the Order of the MOTH

RAYMOND JOHNSON—"The most wicked robber-fly on earth"; also known as the Bald Buzzer

HORNET GANG—Raymond Johnson's henchmen

Publisher's note: This is a work of fiction. Any resemblance to events, locales, or actual bugs (living or dead) is entirely coincidental.

PART I

❧ ONE ❧

Leon Leafwing sang softly to himself as he placed two honey drops on a rose-petal platter.

> *"No one to talk with,*
> *All by myself."*

He filled two buttercups with cherry juice and lit two beeswax candles.

> *"No one to walk with,*
> *But I'm happy on the shelf.*
> *Ain't misbehavin',*
> *I'm savin' my love for you."*

Leon moved two lima-bean-pod chairs close to each other. Then he fluttered to his mica mirror and fluffed up his tiny peach-colored ascot.

> *"I know for certain*
> *The one I love."*

He straightened the lapels on his summer

jacket and flicked a piece of dust from his brownish-orange butterfly wings.

"I'm through with flirtin',
It's just you I'm thinking of.
Ain't misbehavin'…"

Knock, knock, knock.

Leon threw open the door and sang, *"I'm savin' my love for you!"*

The blue gossamer-winged butterfly fluttered excitedly in the twilight. "Oh, Leon, isn't it thrilling?" she cried.

"Well," said Leon, puzzled. "It's actually a rather simple little dinner, darling, but…"

"Oh, you think he just wants to meet us for dinner?" Mimi rushed past Leon into his cabin. "I thought he wanted us for a mission—criminals on the waterfront, smugglers, pirates or something!"

"What?"

"I didn't even know that he was back. Did you? I can't wait to see him!"

"Who?"

"Spider Kane! You think we should leave

soon? I'm not quite sure where Jumbo Night-crawler's is, are you?"

"Wait, wait, wait!" said Leon. "What in the world are you talking about?"

Mimi caught her breath and stared at Leon. "Didn't you get a letter from him?" she said.

"Who? From who?"

"Spider Kane!"

"No, I didn't."

"Oh." Mimi looked confused.

"What letter? What are you talking about?"

"I found this letter in my mailbox just now." Mimi pulled a piece of blue paper from her purse and handed it to Leon. "I was sure you'd gotten one too."

By the flickering candlelight, Leon read the elegant handwriting on the note:

> Dear Mimi,
> At midnight meet me at Jumbo
> Nightcrawler's Supper Club on
> Waterfront Row. Please present this free
> pass to the hostess at the door.
>
> As ever,
> E. M.

The message was signed with the initials of Spider Kane's secret code name, Emperor Moth, and attached to it was a purple ticket with the word *free*. "I wonder why I didn't hear from him," said Leon.

"Did you look in your mailbox today?" Mimi asked.

"Yes, this morning."

"Well, let me check again."

As Mimi fluttered outside, Leon sat on one of his bean-pod chairs and stared at the note. For weeks now he had been living for a night such as this—a night when the mysterious Spider Kane would gather together his five lieutenants and lead them on a mission. Though Spider Kane was known throughout the Cottage Garden as an excellent detective, his Order of the MOTH was a well-kept secret. The abbreviation MOTH stood for Mission: Only to Help, because the spider had formed the band to help those who were unable to help themselves.

"Nothing in your mailbox," said Mimi, returning.

"Maybe he isn't including me on this mission

because I'm the newest and youngest member," Leon said.

"Don't be silly. We don't all have to get our orders at the same time. Spider Kane probably has another plan for you…some really special plan."

"Well, then, maybe I should just go with you anyway," said Leon. "Maybe—"

"I'm afraid not, honey," Mimi interrupted gently. "I've learned from experience that Spider Kane is very specific about his orders."

Leon didn't say anything. He just stared miserably at Mimi's note.

"Look at this wonderful dinner you've made for us!" Mimi said. "I don't have to leave this minute. We have time to eat together."

"I'm not very hungry," Leon mumbled.

"Oh, Leon, don't be sad," Mimi said. "Listen. Let's go visit Rosie and Little Pickles. Maybe they know what's going on."

Rosie and Little Pickles were both ladybug lieutenants in the Order of the MOTH.

"Okay."

"And will you save this lovely dinner for later?"

"I guess so."

Mimi kissed him. "Smile, kiddo," she whispered.

Leon gave her the teeniest smile.

"All right, let's go," she said, and she blew out Leon's two beeswax candles.

Night had fallen when Mimi and Leon left the twig cabin. They stood for a moment beneath the lemon-yellow moon and inhaled the sweet scent of honeysuckle.

"Ready?" Mimi whispered.

"Ready."

The butterflies raised their paper-thin wings and flickered into the balmy night sky. As they sailed above the Cottage Garden, they swooped over darkened patches of wild strawberries, over pasture roses, meadow clover, the Lily Pond, and an old sundial. Just beyond the stone birdbath they glided down to a tiny cottage under a moon-flower vine.

The cottage was the home of Leon's two best friends, Rosie and Little Pickles. When the two tireless ladybugs weren't flying special missions for Spider Kane, they were busy catering Garden parties or building tulip cradles for new Garden babies. Energetic and cheerful, they hated to waste even a second of their waking lives.

But when Leon and Mimi lit down near Rosie and Little Pickles's cottage, they found it completely dark. "Have they gone to bed early for once in their lives?" Mimi asked.

"I can't imagine," said Leon. It puzzled him that no smoke curled from the chimney. And no basket of cookies had been left on the front steps for night-working bugs. When he tapped on the door, it swung open. The cottage seemed very quiet and dark.

"Rosie! Little Pickles!" he called.

But there was no answer.

"Should we just go in?" said Mimi.

"I guess," said Leon, and he cautiously followed Mimi into the living room.

Mimi lit the lantern in the front window. As

she carried it about the cottage, shadows danced on tulip cradles, on dried herbs hanging from the low ceiling, and on leaf tins and flower plates stacked on the white-birch floor.

"Look!" said Leon, pointing to a nutshell bowl filled with mashed apple. On the floor was a tiny pile of apple peelings. "They must have left in the middle of baking."

"What's this?" said Mimi, and she grabbed a blue scrap of paper from the kitchen table. After she read it, she handed it to Leon.

Leon felt his heart sink as he read:

> Dear Rosie and Little Pickles,
> At mid night meet me at Jumbo
> Nightcrawler's Supper Club on
> Waterfront Row. Please present these
> free passes to the hostess at the door.
>
> As ever,
> E. M.

Once again Spider Kane had signed the message with the initials of his secret code name, Emperor Moth. "I wonder why he doesn't want to meet with me," said Leon.

"I don't know, honey," said Mimi.

"You don't think he's changed his mind about making me a member of the Order of the MOTH, do you?" said Leon.

"Oh, no! Never! He's lucky to have you, and he knows it," said Mimi.

"I wonder if he sent a note to the Hawk too."

"I don't know. Do you want to go and find out?"

"Okay." Leon put the note back on the table. And with a sigh, he followed Mimi out of the ladybugs' cottage.

❧ TWO ❧

Hidden near the eastern wall of the Cottage Garden in a patch of meadow rue was the pebble estate of Thomas "the Hawk" Hawkins. Not only was the Hawk an outstanding lieutenant in the Order of the MOTH, he was also the greatest living actor in the moth world. Late at night he could often be found by his fire, reading plays and sometimes speaking the best parts aloud to himself.

But the Hawk's estate was nearly dark when Mimi and Leon arrived. Mimi rang the Hawk's doorbell and called his name, but there was no answer. She rang again.

Suddenly the door swung open. Mimi and Leon saw a horrible face leering at them from the shadows.

"Eek!" Mimi screamed.

"Don't be frightened, my dear," said a smooth, clear voice. "It's only a wooden mask exquisitely carved by the Harlequin Beetles of South America."

Mimi broke into her high little laugh. "Hawk!" she squealed. "You scared me to death!"

The great moth actor lowered the mask to reveal his own craggy, handsome face. "Hello, friends," he said.

Mimi gave the Hawk a big hug. "I'm so glad to see you! We heard your Asian theater tour was a huge success."

"Yes, yes, it was marvelous," said the Hawk. "The bugs turned out in droves to see our little plays."

"Rosie told me that you acquired some priceless treasures, too," said Mimi.

"Ah, she told you about my tapestry?"

"What tapestry?"

"The Moon Shadow Tapestry from the Tailor Ants of Borneo," the Hawk said in a hushed and reverent voice. "Only five of them were ever made. Come, I'll show you…" And he led Mimi and Leon into his house.

A beeswax candle burned in the foyer. The Hawk picked it up and carried it down the hall. As Mimi and Leon followed him, they fluttered past rare objects from all over the world. On other theater tours the Hawk had collected wax statues made by the Honeybees of China, beautiful fans made by the Sun Butterflies of New Guinea, and tin whistles made by the Australian Whistling Moths.

Finally, when they came to the Hawk's bedroom, he pointed to a needlepoint tapestry hanging near his feather bed.

"Oh! It's incredible!" breathed Mimi.

Leon wondered what the big fuss was about. The tapestry looked like an old rug with a picture of a couple of ants hugging in the moonlight.

"Don't let its simplicity fool you," said the Hawk, as if he had read Leon's mind. "The craftsmanship is unequaled anywhere in the world. You can't imagine my joy when I came upon it in a tiny shop in the hills of Borneo. And to think I got it for only a song."

"How fabulous!" said Mimi. "What song did you sing?"

"'Ducks on the Millpond,'" said the Hawk.

Mimi laughed her high little laugh again. "I'm not surprised they gave it to you," she said. "You have such a lovely voice."

Leon felt a pang of jealousy. Mimi had always admired *his* singing voice.

"So what are you two up to?" said the Hawk.

"Oh! I got a letter today from Spider Kane," said Mimi. "So did Rosie and Little Pickles. He wants us to meet him at midnight on Waterfront Row."

"Marvelous!" said the Hawk. "I got a message

19

from old E. M. myself. I was just getting ready to leave. Shall we all go together?"

"Well — I — " stammered Leon.

"Leon didn't get a note, Hawk," said Mimi quickly. "We can't figure out why. Do you know? Have you spoken to Mr. Kane?"

"No, but I'm sure Spy plans to include you in this new mission of his, Leon."

"How do you know?"

"He sent me a postcard recently. He's been in the North Country, you know, meeting with the United Ant Charities. But he wrote that as soon as he got back, he was going to call all of us together for an assignment — and he definitely included you."

"He did?"

"Of course. I'll prove it to you." The Hawk picked up a postcard from his dresser. Then he put on his reading glasses and read aloud:

> *"My dear Hawk,*
> *I'm so glad to hear about your safe*
> *return — and your wonderful treasure.*
> *What a steal! Those ants are amazing,*

aren't they? Please tell Rosie, Little
Pickles, Mimi, and Lieutenant Leafwing
that as soon as I'm back from my trip, I'll
be calling together our gang of six. After
we celebrate your success, I'll outline our
next little caper.

> *As ever,*
> *E. M."*

The Hawk took off his glasses and smiled at Leon. "You see?" he said. "Spider Kane hasn't forgotten *Lieutenant Leafwing.*"

"Then why didn't he invite me to the supper club tonight?" said Leon.

"I can't answer that, dear boy. But I do know that Spy never does anything without a good reason. Trust him."

"I guess you're right," said Leon, sighing.

The Hawk glanced at his pocket watch. Then he put on his fedora. "Well, we'd better be going or we'll be late...It's a bit of a journey to the waterfront."

Mimi fluttered to Leon's side and gave him a soft butterfly kiss. "If we don't fly off on a mission,

I'll come straight to your house after the meeting and tell you all about it, okay?"

"Okay," whispered Leon.

"Save that wonderful dinner you prepared for us."

"You bet," said Leon, trying to sound cheerful.

"*Au revoir,* my friend," said the Hawk gently. He tipped his fedora. Then he opened his wings and swept Mimi out the back door.

After Leon left the Hawk's estate, he flew as fast as he could over the Cottage Garden back to his twig cabin in the Wildflower Woods.

When he got home, he searched everywhere for his own blue note from Spider Kane. Maybe the wind had blown it out of his mailbox. Maybe it had fallen behind a hedge or was floating in his hickory rain barrel.

But there was no note. At last Leon went inside and lit his candles. Then he sat in his twig rocker and waited for Mimi.

As he rocked, Leon couldn't help picturing

his girlfriend sitting close to the handsome Hawk in a dark music club on Waterfront Row. And Rosie and Little Pickles, his two best friends, were with them! He pictured all of them receiving orders from Spider Kane while the band played and bugs danced and a singer sang about faraway places. It was almost more than he could bear.

Finally, before dawn, Leon washed the honey drops off his rose-petal platter. He poured the cherry juice back into an acorn jug. He took off his peach-colored ascot and his summer jacket. Then he blew out his candles.

As Leon lay on his pine-needle bed in the dark, he listened longingly to the night winds rustling the leaves outside. His heart was so heavy that when he finally fell asleep, he dreamed he was sinking like a stone to the bottom of the Garden Creek.

❧ THREE ❧

As soon as Leon woke up, he dashed next door to Mimi's burrow under the May-apple. When she didn't answer his knock, he peeked inside her front window. The little burrow looked as tidy as ever. A moss coverlet lay neatly on Mimi's straw bed. The bare earthen floor was swept smooth and clean. But there was no sign Mimi had returned from her meeting with Spider Kane.

Back home, Leon perched on his front step and watched for his gossamer-winged girlfriend. He also wistfully kept an eye out for Spider Kane. He pictured the elegant captain dressed in his gray cape, limping down the road toward the cabin. Two of the spider's legs had been wounded in the Mosquito Wars. But that had not prevented him from traveling all over the world investigating crimes or leading the Order of the MOTH, as well as playing jazz clarinet and directing theatrical productions.

Leon waited all morning, but Mimi never

came. Finally in the early afternoon he decided to find out if Rosie, Little Pickles, or the Hawk had returned from the meeting with Spider Kane. In the hazy, hot sunlight he flew across the Cottage Garden to the Hawk's pebble estate. When he found no one at home, he hurried to the ladybugs' cottage. But just as he'd expected, he found no one there, either.

When Leon returned home, he was too forlorn to putter in his garden or make a good dinner. He lay down on his pine bed and stared mournfully out the window.

It wasn't until the sun was going down that he spied a butterfly in the distance winging toward his cabin. Joy surged through him as he zipped out the door to greet Mimi. "Darling!" he shouted.

"Sonny!" answered the butterfly.

Leon moaned with disappointment. Not his darling Mimi, but his mother was fluttering toward him. La Mère Leafwing was wearing an orange kimono with an ostrich fern draped around her neck. She was carrying her tiny companion, Walter Dogtick. The barefoot tick wore his usual ill-fitting old coat.

"Wally and I are on our way to dinner, dearie," said La Mère, lighting down in Leon's yard. "We thought you might like to join us."

"No thanks, Mom," said Leon.

"Oh, sonny, I never see you anymore. Not since you insisted on getting your own place next to that tacky old butterfly," said La Mère. La Mère was quite jealous of Mimi and took every opportunity to insult her. She often brought up the fact that Mimi was a bit older than Leon.

"Moth-er…" warned Leon.

"Forgive me, forgive me!" La Mère said insincerely. "But you know, I'm lonely, dearie. I have no chums now except Wally." La Mère had been without friends ever since she'd had a falling-out with the Women's Bug Club.

"I know that, Mother. I feel bad about that. But—"

"Oh, don't worry about me!" interrupted La Mère. "But aren't you even slightly interested in why we're making a visit to Waterfront Row?"

"Waterfront Row?"

"Yes, we're going to Jumbo Nightcrawler's Supper Club."

"Jumbo Nightcrawler's Supper Club?"

"Yes, indeedy," said La Mère. "Wally and I are winging it to the wild side!"

"Dat's right, Pupa," said Walter Dogtick, calling La Mère by her childhood name. The two had grown up next to each other in the Goatweed Patch.

"But why—why are you going to Jumbo Nightcrawler's?" stammered Leon.

"Well, actually I received this rather odd invitation." La Mère handed a blue note to Leon and winked. "I think I have a secret admirer," she said.

Leon unfolded the paper and read:

Dear L. Leafwing,

*At midnight meet me at Jumbo
Nightcrawler's Supper Club on
Waterfront Row. Please present this free
pass to the hostess at the door.*

As ever,
E. M.

"Oh! Oh! This is *my* note!" Leon shrieked.

"I beg your pardon?" said La Mère.

"This is mine! Mine! I'm sure of it! This was meant for me!" Leon was so excited he could barely contain himself.

"What are you talking about?" said La Mère huffily. "You know this E. M.?"

"He's—he's—" Leon sputtered. He couldn't reveal Spider Kane's secret code name to anyone, not even his own mother. "I'm—I'm not sure who he is," he said, "but I am sure this note was meant for me!"

"Well, I'm not so sure," said La Mère, pulling her ostrich fern about her.

"No, Mom, listen. This note is mine. Trust me. See, L. Leafwing could mean Leon Leafwing just as easily as La Mère Leafwing!"

"Yes, but it was sent to *my* address, dearie!" said La Mère, trying to snatch the note from Leon.

"I know, but that must have been a mistake. When did you find this in your mailbox?"

"This morning."

"Did you look in your mailbox yesterday?"

La Mère thought for a moment, then said, "No. I haven't been getting much mail lately." She sniffed pathetically.

"Oh, darn." Leon could have wept with disappointment. He was almost certain he was supposed to have received his note yesterday with all the others.

"Well, all you have to do is write me, dearie," said La Mère, misunderstanding Leon's disappointment.

"Yes, I know, Mother." Leon folded the note and put it in his pocket. Then he heaved a big sigh. "Well, can I go with you?" he said, hoping against hope that just maybe Spider Kane meant to meet with him alone that night.

"Of course!" said La Mère. "Let's *all* wing it to the wild side!"

❧ FOUR ❧

The Garden Creek ran along the southern border of the Cottage Garden. Hidden along its shore was the strange nightlife of Waterfront Row. From dusk until dawn night bugs and worms haunted the music clubs beneath the wild oats and foxtail grass.

Dogtick rode on La Mère's back, and Leon followed as they wove their way past dancing gnats rising and falling in the misty twilight. Oil lamps glowed in the leaf shanties that dotted the tiny hills and hollows around the creek.

Finally they let down in the cinnamon grass near Waterfront Row. "Where's Jumbo Nightcrawler's?" Leon asked.

"Follow me," said Dogtick, and he crept away into the mist.

La Mère and Leon fluttered after Dogtick until they came to the creek's edge. Tiny waves lapped against the soggy bank, and torches lit the entrance to a mud cavern.

"What a spooky place," said La Mère. "I hope the food's good."

"Precious, you'll be lucky if it's not *alive!*" said Dogtick.

"Oooooh!" squealed La Mère.

Inside, the club was jammed.

"May I help you?" said a husky voice. A glamorous-looking bee was standing by the door. She wore a long purple dress with a lilac cape, a blond wig, and rose-tinted glasses. Around her neck was a gold chain with a gold key.

"I believe I'm supposed to present you with this free pass," said La Mère, holding out her ticket.

The bee looked startled. Then she smiled. "Oh, yes, yes," she said. "Thank you."

"How 'bout making that pass good for all three of us, sweetheart?" said Dogtick, winking.

"Of course," said the bee. "Follow me."

As the bee led them across the sawdust dance floor, Dogtick said, "Who's playing tonight, sweetheart?"

"I'll be at the piano," said the bee. "And my friend, Johnny St. Claire, will be playing the trumpet."

"And your name, sweetheart?" said Dogtick.

"Saratoga," she said. "Saratoga D'Bee."

"Ah, lookin' forward to hearing ya, Ms. D'Bee," said Dogtick. "Nice hairdo you got there."

The bee smiled with embarrassment. "Thank you," she said. "Now, why don't you sit here? Your waiter will be right with you."

"Okey-dokey," said Dogtick.

After Saratoga D'Bee left them, La Mère looked around the club. "Let's all keep an eye out for this mysterious E. M.," she said.

But Leon was already desperately searching the smoky, dimly lit room for Spider Kane. Dragonflies and dance flies lined the juice bar on the side wall. Moths and caterpillars sat at tables or milled about the dance floor. Hornets and lightning bugs careened overhead.

But just as he expected, there was no sign of Spider Kane. Leon was sure that the members of the Order of the MOTH were all off on some great adventure. What rotten luck—not only had Leon's note been delivered to the wrong address, it had been discovered on the wrong day. He

32

could hardly stand it.

Suddenly the crowd began to clap.

"Ooooh! Look at that big old thing!" said La Mère.

An enormous worm was moving across the stage, heading toward the microphone. He wore a panama hat, a white silk vest, and a flowered tie. A cigar was stuck in his mouth, and smoke curled up into the pink spotlight over his head.

"The Fat Worm himself," said Dogtick.

Jumbo Nightcrawler stood under the spotlight and surveyed the crowd through the haze of his cigar smoke. "Good evening, ladies and gentlemen," he said in a low, growly voice. "It is indeed a great pleasure to have you here in my club this fine summer evening. You bugs are looking mighty good out there tonight. Mighty good."

The bugs applauded for themselves.

"I'd like to remind y'all that tomorrow night we're hosting our annual talent show. Ms. D'Bee will be auditioning entries all afternoon. Then next weekend I'll be master of ceremonies at the

Lightning Bug Races. Of course, y'all know what I always say to start the race, don't you? *Ready, set, glow!*"

The audience moaned as the fat worm jiggled with laughter. "Okay, okay, I apologize. But now I'd like y'all to give a big round of applause for that powerful musical duo—our own Mr. Johnny St. Claire and your lovely hostess this evening, Ms. Saratoga D'Bee!"

A tuxedo-clad housefly carrying a shiny trumpet buzzed onto the stage. Following him was Saratoga D'Bee, the club's glamorous hostess. As the two performers bowed, the bugs clapped and whooped and pounded on the tables.

"The crowd is hot tonight," said Dogtick.

Saratoga sat at her piano. Then she leaned toward her mike and said in her husky voice, "I've got a new song I'd like to try out on y'all. Are you ready to go wild?"

"Yay!" the crowd screamed.

"Good," said Saratoga D'Bee. "Then let's all do the Bee House Stomp!"

Johnny St. Claire began tooting his horn, and Saratoga D'Bee began plunking her piano. As they played, bugs of all shapes and sizes swarmed onto the dance floor. The crowd moved their bodies in every possible way—they twisted, shimmied, slithered, buzzed, and stomped.

Leon stared unhappily at the crowd. Even the joyful music and rowdy atmosphere could not ease his terrible disappointment at being left behind by the Order of the MOTH.

Saratoga D'Bee began to sing:

> *"Policeman, policeman, don't catch me!*
> *Catch that bug in the ostrich fern.*
> *She took the money, I took none;*
> *Put her in the bee house, just for fun."*

Johnny St. Claire played a trumpet solo, puffing out his cheeks like tiny balloons. Saratoga answered with a long, steady piano roll. Then they played together—plunking and tooting. The piano rocked, and the platform swayed. An oil lamp on the mud wall cast great moving shadows of all the bugs doing the Bee House Stomp.

When the song ended, Saratoga D'Bee threw back her head and hollered, "Shoo fly!" And someone blew out the light.

In the dark the audience went wild, screaming and clapping.

When the noise finally died down, Dogtick cried, "That was great! Beautiful! Wasn't it, precious?"

But there was no answer. When the oil lamp flickered back on, Leon saw that his mother was not in her seat.

"Pupa?" Dogtick said. "Pupa?" He turned to Leon. "Where's your mother at?"

"I don't know," said Leon. "Maybe she stepped out for some air. I'll go check."

As Johnny St. Claire began playing a mournful solo, Leon wove his way through the slow-dancing crowd toward the door.

Just as he fluttered into the cool, damp night, a low-pitched voice came from behind him. "Wait."

Leon turned and saw a weird-looking character in a black hooded cloak. The creature's face was completely covered. As it moved jerkily toward him, Leon gasped and fled toward the water. But the creature came after him.

As Leon started to lift off into the weeds beside the creek, he caught his wing in a clump of bristle grass. He shook himself furiously, trying to get free. Suddenly the hooded monster leaped out of nowhere and landed on top of him.

Leon fought with all his might as the creature held on to him and whisked him into the bulrushes. "Help!" Leon screamed. "Help!"

"Be still!" his captor said in a deep, velvety voice. "Be still!"

"Spider Kane!" said Leon.

✺ FIVE ✺

"Shhh!" whispered Spider Kane.

"What—?" said Leon.

"Shhh! We have no time to lose. We have to find your mother. I need you to carry me into the air!"

"But—"

"Don't ask questions!" said Spider Kane as he quickly tied a cobweb thread to the butterfly. "Fly now! Fly!" he said.

In a daze Leon lifted off the ground into the misty dark. Spider Kane dangled below him as the two glided over the clubs on the mud bank— the Glowworm, Leo "Buzzy" Cicada's, the Hornflower Inn, and the King Cricket Casino.

Insect songs and peeper calls mingled with the music coming from the dance bands. Suave, neatly dressed mosquitoes hummed through the mist. Fireflies flashed mysterious signals to one another. And darkling beetles scuttled along the shore.

But Leon saw no sign of a matronly butterfly in an orange kimono. And he couldn't imagine why in the world Spider Kane had lunged out of the dark, searching for La Mère.

Suddenly Leon felt a tug. As he lit down on the lawn of the King Cricket Casino, he heard the *click, click, wheep, wheep* of the Cricket Brothers' Quartet.

"Quick, fly me over the creek and back," said Spider Kane. "They might have taken her by boat."

"Who?"

"I'll explain later. Hurry! Go!"

Leon lifted off the ground again and fluttered over the dark water, searching for small watercraft. *They might have taken her by boat.* What did that awful-sounding statement mean?

Leon felt another tug. Then he heard Spider Kane call, "Go back!"

When they had landed near Jumbo Nightcrawler's, Spider Kane started limping down the Bug Fishing Pier, which stretched into the creek. Finally he came to a halt and peered out over the water with a tiny reed telescope.

"What do you see?" Leon cried.

Spider Kane slowly lowered the telescope. "Absolutely nothing," he said, sighing.

"Where's my mother? What happened to her?" said Leon.

"I'm afraid she has been kidnapped," said Spider Kane.

"Kidnapped? By who?" gasped Leon.

"I'm not sure. It was quite dark, but I heard her cry out as several flying creatures whisked her out of the club."

"Flying creatures?" said Leon.

"Yes. Perhaps hornets...I wonder now if they might be related to the larger mystery that I am working on."

"Oh, you—you mean the mystery that made you send for everyone?" said Leon.

"I beg your pardon?"

"Is that why you sent us all those blue notes? Because of this larger mystery you're working on? Where is everyone? Where's Mimi and—"

"Wait," said Spider Kane. "What blue notes?"

"The blue notes that told us to meet you at Jumbo Nightcrawler's. Mine went to my mother, so I didn't—"

Suddenly Spider Kane grabbed Leon and held him firmly. "Stop, stop," he said. "Tell me *exactly* what you're talking about."

"I'm—I'm talking about the blue notes you sent to all the members of the Order of the

MOTH!" said Leon. "I got mine today. Did you mean for me to meet you today? Or yesterday with the others?"

"Leon! Where are the others now?" said Spider Kane.

"I don't know. They never came home. Don't—don't you know where they are?"

Spider Kane snarled with fury. Then he flung his black cloak around him and stalked off the Bug Fishing Pier.

Leon was overcome with terror. He'd never seen the spider in such a rage. He rushed after him. "What's wrong?" he cried. "What's wrong? Where is everyone?"

Spider Kane brought himself under control. Then he spoke in a low voice. "I don't know where they are," he said. "I only returned to the Garden this afternoon. All I know is that *I did not send any blue notes to anyone.*"

SIX

Leon stared at Spider Kane. Finally he breathed, "Then—then why are you here tonight?"

"While I was away, I was asked to investigate a waterfront crime," said Spider Kane. "I was going to call the Order of the MOTH together soon to help me. But first I wanted to do a little snooping on my own. However, it now seems someone has discovered my plan—and grabbed my lieutenants before I could gather them together."

"What?" said Leon, close to hysteria. "You mean Mimi—"

Suddenly a plaintive cry came from nearby. "Pupa? Pupa?"

"Good heavens," said Spider Kane, and he limped into the bulrushes as Walter Dogtick stumbled into view.

In the circle of light thrown by the supper club's torches, the tick looked lost. "Where's Pupa?" he asked, blinking at Leon.

"I don't know, Wally!"

"Where's she at?" said Dogtick.

"I *said* I don't know, Wally. I don't know!"

"You think she ran off with that E. M.?"

"No, Wally. Please, leave me alone!"

"I just wanted her to have a nice time," Dogtick said mournfully.

"I know, Wally. Now go away, please."

"Pupa? Pupa?" Dogtick called as he stumbled away into the night.

Fear and dread filled Leon as he stared after Dogtick. Where *was* his mother? Where was Mimi? Rosie? Little Pickles? The Hawk? What was going on? "Mr. Kane!" he said in a loud whisper.

Shadows of drift worms moved eerily along the foggy shore as the weeping strains of Johnny St. Claire's trumpet floated through the thick night air.

"Mr. Kane!" cried Leon.

"Here I am," said Spider Kane, limping out of the bulrushes. "Come, let's go back to my place. We must figure this out."

"Y-yes," said Leon, trembling.

Spider Kane attached a cobweb thread to the butterfly again. As they flew away from Waterfront Row, Walter Dogtick's lonely cry could be heard coming through the mist. "Pupa! Pupa!"

PART II

❧ SEVEN ❧

Leon and Spider Kane flew through the night to a crumbling stone wall on the south side of the Cottage Garden. After they had landed in the tall grass, the spider led the way through a tunnel in the wall to his elegant chambers.

Leon was still trembling with shock as Spider Kane lit the candelabra on his mantel and made a fire in his fireplace. When the dancing flames were casting shadows on the chalky walls, the spider turned to Leon. "Pull your chair close to the fire, son," he said. "It's a little chilly in here, isn't it?"

Leon did as he was told. Spider Kane changed into his paisley dressing gown and poured cherry juice into two touch-me-not goblets. After he had served Leon, he took out his briarwood pipe.

Spider Kane puffed silently for a moment, then said, "Now, let's go over this entire business one step at a time. First, the blue notes. What exactly did each note say?"

"I have the one my mother received." Leon reached in his pocket and pulled out the note that had been sent to La Mère. "The others say exactly the same thing," he said.

"Ah…let me see," said Spider Kane, taking the note from him. "Yes, that certainly is a good imitation of my handwriting. And somehow the forger knew my secret signature. Tell me—was *midnight* spelled as two words in all the notes that you saw?"

"Yes, I think so."

"And all the notes included a free pass to the club?"

"Yes."

"Hmm. What else can you tell me?"

Leon described his visit to Rosie and Little Pickles's cottage. "It was as if they'd dropped everything and rushed away," he said. "They even left mashed apple sitting in a nutshell bowl and apple peelings on the floor."

"Good heavens." The spider heaved a sigh. "Well, as I said before, I only returned to the Garden this afternoon. I've been in the North Country, meeting with the United Ant Charities. They have a case they'd like me to solve. As I said, I fully intended to enlist the assistance of the Order of the MOTH. But first I wanted to do a little investigating on my own."

"But why were you at Jumbo Nightcrawler's tonight?" said Leon.

"I was scouting for clues to the ant case. I planned to visit all the music clubs and keep my ears open for gossip about crimes that had taken place recently on the creek. The fact that I happened to be at Jumbo's to witness your mother's capture was pure coincidence."

Spider Kane looked again at the blue note that had been sent to La Mère. "So, whoever sent this note knew my secret signature..." His eyes closed for a moment. Then suddenly they shot open. "Aha!" he whispered fiercely. "Yes. Yes!"

"Yes what?" cried Leon.

"Wait!" Spider Kane jumped up, then limped across the room to his coat rack and grabbed a newspaper clipping from the pocket of his gray traveling cloak. "I want to read you an article from last week's *Garden Times*," he said. "It concerns the case I was starting to investigate on the waterfront." Then he read out loud:

More Bad News for the Ants

For ages, on the Atacama Desert of Chile, Harvester Ants have mined particles of fine gold. The hardworking, selfless ants have always kept only a tiny portion of the gold for themselves. The rest they send to the UAC (United Ant Charities). The UAC then sends the gold to a needy colony somewhere in the world. Recently, the Ant Kingdom in the Cottage Garden was chosen to receive the UAC's charity. As everyone knows, the Ant Kingdom suffered devastation from the spring-thaw mud slides this year. But as the UAC cargo ship was sailing down the Garden Creek, the gold was quietly stolen in the night. The sailor ant guarding the gold vanished also. It's believed that he was either taken hostage or thrown overboard. Sadly, the Ant Kingdom has lost out again.

When he had finished reading, Spider Kane sat down, relit his pipe, and stared at the fire.

Leon was confused. "I—I don't think we can worry about the ants until we find the other members of the Order of the MOTH," he said.

Spider Kane kept staring at his fire, deep in thought.

"Mr. Kane?"

When Spider Kane looked at Leon, his eyes were burning. "I could be wrong, Lieutenant, but I have a suspicion there's a connection between this mystery"—he rattled the newspaper clipping—"and the disappearances of our friends and loved ones."

"Wh-why?" asked Leon.

"Before I voice my suspicions, I need to study things a bit more." The spider stood. "Perhaps you should leave now, Leon, and get some rest. I have an important assignment for you tomorrow."

"You do? What?"

"I want you to go to the Hawk's house and Rosie's cottage and find their blue notes for me. But most important, when you're in the Hawk's house, search carefully for a postcard I sent him from the North Country last week."

"Oh, yes. He read that card to me."

"Excellent. I'm glad he saved it. Find it, please, and bring it to me."

"Yes, sir."

"Now go directly home," said Spider Kane as he accompanied Leon to the entrance of his chamber. "And be very careful, Lieutenant. We're not sure *who* or *what* we're dealing with."

There was no moonlight and no starlight. As Leon lifted into the sky, the coal-black dark trembled with mysterious sounds. *We're not sure who or what we're dealing with*. Terrified, Leon flew home as fast as he could.

The butterfly was still in a panic when he lit down at his twig cabin in the Wildflower Woods. As he unlocked his door, the wind picked up speed and seemed to whisper, *They're coming, they're coming*.

Leon rushed inside. After he locked his door, he pushed his jelly cupboard against it. Then without even lighting a candle, he dived into his soft, leafy bed.

As the wind moaned outside, Leon tried to imagine what had happened to Mimi, Rosie, Little Pickles, the Hawk, and his mother. He was afraid that any moment La Mère's kidnappers might burst into his house and snatch him, too.

Leon was so distraught that several times he got up and fluttered about the tiny one-room cabin. Finally he drove away his bad thoughts by pulling his covers over his head and imagining he was surrounded by a thick, protective butterfly cocoon.

❧ EIGHT ❧

Leon woke as soon as the first morning light filtered into his cabin. He immediately rushed next door to Mimi's. Peering through her window, he prayed that last night had been a bad dream. But there was no sign Mimi had returned to her little burrow.

With a heavy heart, Leon prepared to set off for the Hawk's estate to find Spider Kane's postcard. Just as he lifted into the hazy morning sky he heard cries of "Leon! Leon!"

Leon fluttered back to the ground and watched Walter Dogtick wobble toward him. The old tick looked more ill-kempt than ever. His coat was dragging along the ground, and his eyes were red and bleary. "Where's your mother at, Leon?" he cried. "Where?"

"I don't know, Wally."

"She didn't go back home to the Goatweed Patch. She didn't visit the Flowerpot District. No one's seen her, Leon. Did she run away with that E. M.?"

"No, absolutely not, Wally. E. M. is a friend of mine. I've talked to him. He hasn't seen her."

"Well, why did he tell her to meet him at Jumbo Nightcrawler's?"

"He didn't, Wally. That was a trick."

"A trick? Whadya mean? Who tricked her?"

Leon was afraid to tell Dogtick about the flying creatures taking La Mère away. It was all too confusing at this point. "I don't know, Wally."

"Maybe she was playing a trick on me," said Dogtick. "Maybe she wanted to escape from me because I'm so grubby."

"No, Wally, no."

"Why not?" said the tick. "I'd run away from me too, if I could." And with a self-loathing moan, Dogtick crept off into the Wildflower Woods.

"Wally, don't blame yourself!" called Leon. "Wally!"

But Walter Dogtick kept going without looking back.

When he arrived at the Hawk's estate, Leon slipped through the door and fluttered down the hall. He passed the wax statues from China and the fans from New Guinea.

Then in the Hawk's bedroom, he stared for a moment at the rare Moon Shadow Tapestry from Borneo. The little ants embracing in the moonlight reminded him of himself and Mimi. "Oh, darling, where are you?" he whispered tearfully.

Leon finally turned away from the tapestry and began searching for the Hawk's blue note and the postcard Spider Kane had sent the moth from the North Country. Leon found them both on the dresser. Just as he put them in his pocket, he heard an ominous sound—*Hmmmmmmmm*.

Leon fluttered to a corner. Then he protected himself as his leafwing ancestors had done for eons: he folded his wings above his back, making himself look like a dead leaf.

Hmmmmmmmm.

Leon opened one eye and nearly fainted with horror. Four hornets were gliding down the Hawk's hallway. A fat hornet paused to look behind the South American masks. A skinny hornet looked under the New Guinea fans. A tall hornet shook the Chinese statues. A short hornet studied the Moon Shadow Tapestry.

"It ain't here, fellas," said the tall one.

"The boss says we gotta find it," said the skinny one.

"He'll flip out if we don't," said the short one.

"Benny's right, it ain't here," said the fat one. "Let's beat it."

Then the four hornets zipped out the back door.

When the coast was clear, Leon fled from the lonely mansion as fast as he could. As he sailed over the Cottage Garden, he wondered why the hornets had been snooping about the Hawk's estate. Who was the "boss" they had spoken of? And what had he ordered them to find? Leon was desperate to tell Spider Kane about the four prowlers, but first he had to retrieve Rosie and Little Pickles's blue note.

When Leon entered the ladybugs' cottage under the moonflower vine, he found it more forlorn than ever. The little clay oven was not sending out its usual odors of cinnamon and nutmeg. The air was not filled with the sounds of ladybug laughter. Dust had gathered everywhere. The mashed apple in the nutshell bowl had turned dark brown.

Leon found the blue note on the kitchen

table. Just as he grabbed it, he heard that noise again. *Hmmmmmmmm.*

Leon quickly hid behind the kitchen table. Once again, he folded his wings above his back to make himself look like a dead leaf. Then as he held his breath, he saw the same four hornets glide through the front door.

The hornets began prowling about the sitting room. The skinny one looked under the corn-husk sofa. The fat one peered inside the pie safe. The tall one looked inside the tiny clay oven. The short one examined the tulip cradles.

Suddenly there was a noise outside.

"Hey, someone's coming!" said the thin one.

"Let's get outta here!" said the fat one.

"Go! Get! Beat it!" said the tall one.

"Move!" said the short one.

The four hornets scooted out the front door just as the back door opened. Leon stayed frozen to the spot, wondering what awful creature was going to break into the cottage next.

Flick-flack, flick-flack came the sound of wing strokes. The noise was wonderfully familiar!

"Little Pickles!" Leon cried as a tiny, plump ladybug wearing a red shawl flickered into the kitchen.

"Leon! You scared me to death! What are you doing here?" said Little Pickles.

"What are you doing here?" Leon said.

"Oh, I had to take care of Aunt Lila. Her house caught fire Saturday. And she lost nearly everything. I helped her get situated with her sister, Bootie. See, Bootie lives in —"

"Excuse me, Little Pickles," Leon interrupted. "But where's Rosie? Did she go with you?"

"No. Isn't Rosie back yet?" said the ladybug, glancing about.

"Where is she, Little Pickles? When did you see her last?"

"Oh. The day before yesterday. She left to cater a party. Then she was going to meet Mr. Kane at Jumbo Nightcrawler's Supper Club. I was supposed to join her there at midnight. But in the middle of baking, I got word about Aunt Lila. Oh, horrors," said Little Pickles as she stared at the nutshell bowl filled with apple.

"What a mess..." She began to tidy up.

"Wait, wait a minute," said Leon. His voice was shaking. "Listen to me, Little Pickles."

The ladybug took one look at the butterfly and dropped her apron.

"Come in here," Leon said, and he led Little Pickles into the front room. He quickly peeked out the window to make sure the hornets were not outside. Then he pulled the curtains shut and lit down next to the ladybug on the sofa.

"I have some bad news..." he began. He told her all about the kidnapping of La Mère. He told her about running into Spider Kane. He told her about all the blue notes being fakes. He told her about the hornet intruders. And last of all, he told her that Rosie and the others had not been seen for two days.

When he finished, Little Pickles looked stunned. "You—you mean Rosie's disappeared?"

Leon nodded sorrowfully.

"And you think she and the others might have been captured like your mother? By those awful hornets?"

"Maybe," said Leon.

"Oh." Little Pickles stared at him with wide, desperate eyes. "I—I feel like screaming," she said.

"Go ahead and scream, Miss Pickles," said a deep, velvety voice. Then Spider Kane limped through the open back door into the sitting room.

"Oh, Mr. Kane!" said Little Pickles. But instead of screaming, she burst into tears.

❧ NINE ❧

"There, there," said Spider Kane as he patted the distraught ladybug on the back. "I thought I would find you here, Miss Pickles. When I reviewed the evidence of your departure, I realized you would never leave mashed apple in a bowl or apple peelings on the floor. Unless, of course, you were rushing off to help someone in immediate danger. If you'd left to join me on a mission, you'd surely have cleaned your cottage first."

"That's true," said Little Pickles, sniffing. "I wanted to bake a pie for everyone and clean the cottage before I joined you on the mission. But then I got word about Aunt Lila's fire. See, she lost—"

"Excuse me for interrupting, Little Pickles," said Leon. "But I have to tell Mr. Kane something important!"

"Indeed? What?" said the spider.

"Four hornets broke into the Hawk's place! Then they came over here!" Leon went on to explain about the four prowlers in the Hawk's estate and Little Pickles's cottage.

"And that's all you can remember of their conversation?" said Spider Kane.

"Yes," said Leon. "I just remember one of them saying, 'The boss says we gotta find it.' And another saying, 'He'll flip out if we don't.'"

Spider Kane stood and began pacing about the living room, lost in thought.

"Who's their boss?" asked Little Pickles.

Spider Kane shook his head absently, then paused to glance out the window. "Good heavens," he exclaimed. "Someone else is heading this way now. I believe it's—yes, it is—it's the singer from Jumbo Nightcrawler's."

"Saratoga D'Bee?" said Leon.

"Yes. Quick, Leon, hide with me," said Spider Kane. "Miss Pickles, the bee must be coming to see you. Do not reveal *any*—I repeat, any—information to her. Say as little as possible. Let her do all the talking."

"Yes, sir." The tiny ladybug quickly pulled herself out of her grief and assumed a military air.

"Into the kitchen, Leon—" said Spider Kane. And he hurriedly led the butterfly into the kitchen, where they hid behind the cream-colored curtains.

A moment later, Leon heard a knock at the front door. Then he heard Little Pickles say, "Yes?"

"Are you Miss Little Pickles?" came a husky-sounding voice.

"Yes."

"My name is Saratoga D'Bee. I must talk to

you. I have a terrible confession to make. May I come in?"

"Yes."

Leon heard the door close. Then he heard the buzzing and flick-flacking of wings. He peeked out from behind the kitchen curtain just long enough to see the bee and the ladybug light down on the sofa.

Wearing a black silk cape, her rose-tinted glasses, and her blond wig, Saratoga D'Bee was fiddling nervously with the gold key that dangled from the chain around her neck. When she looked up at Little Pickles, Leon quickly hid behind the curtain again.

"I had to do it," the bee suddenly blurted out. "I didn't want to, but I had to! He made me."

"Yes?" said Little Pickles.

"Yes. See, I helped your friends get captured, Miss Pickles. I found out who they were when I collected their free passes at the door—he planned it so they'd be the only ones with free passes, of course. And then I had to identify all of them to the hornets with my songs."

"Yes?" said Little Pickles.

"Oh, yes, I'm so disgusted with myself," said the bee. "Take the leafwing, for instance. She was wearing this tacky ostrich fern, so I put it in my song:

> *'Policeman, policeman, don't catch me!*
> *Catch that bug in the ostrich fern.*
> *She took the money, I took none;*
> *Put her in the bee house, just for fun.'*

The 'ostrich fern' tipped off his gang of hornets. So when the lights went out, they grabbed her and took her off."

"Yes?" said Little Pickles.

"Yes! And the same thing happened to the others the night before. I sang about the moth's fedora. I sang about the butterfly's blue wings. I sang about the ladybug's hand-knitted shawl. Then they each got taken away too."

"Ye-es." Little Pickles's voice wobbled a bit. But she cleared her throat.

"Oh, please believe me when I say I didn't want to help him! He forced me, see? But they're all okay, I promise you!" said the bee.

"Only I can't tell you where they are because I don't have any idea where they are."

"Yes?" said Little Pickles.

"Yes!" said the bee. "And please don't ask me who *he* is. I can't tell you that, either. He'd seek terrible revenge if he ever found out that I squealed on him."

"Yes?"

"Oh, yes, he's very wicked, Miss Pickles. You're probably wondering how I got hooked up with a creep like that in the first place. See, I used to be his girlfriend. I was just a mixed-up young thing. But when I got smart, I escaped to the waterfront and got a job at Jumbo Nightcrawler's. Jumbo's a doll. Johnny St. Claire is too. So when I started singing there, I felt like I'd found my true home at last."

"Yes," said Little Pickles.

"Everything was going great until the creep found me. He wanted me to help him kidnap your friends. He threatened to tell Jumbo about my past and get me fired. But worse, he threatened—"

"Yes?" said Little Pickles.

"To harm my three little bees. I—I have three adorable little bees, Miss Pickles. They're staying with my mother now. Let me show you their picture..."

"Yes," said Little Pickles.

"See...that's Bubba, Natalie, and—and my baby, Mike." Leon heard the bee sniff, then blow her nose. He thought he heard Little Pickles sniffling too.

"You got a good heart, Miss Pickles," said the bee in her husky voice.

"Yes."

"So you see why I'm so afraid of him? You see why I went along with him and sang all those dreadful songs that identified his victims to the hornets?"

"Yes," said Little Pickles.

"Thank you for understanding," said the bee. "But now I feel so guilty and dreadful. We got to work together to get your friends free and to get this creep outta our lives for good!"

"Yes!" said Little Pickles.

"There's only one thing that will send him packing," said the bee. "He keeps talking about gold. He keeps talking about someone named E. M. It seems your friends—and this E. M. character—know about some shipment of gold that he meant to steal for himself. I don't know what he's talking about. But if you know, could you bring this gold to me so I could give it to him? We've got to do something to help your friends. And to help keep my Bubba, Natalie, and Baby Mike from his clutches—" The bee burst into hysterical crying.

"Yes, yes, yes," said Little Pickles soothingly.

"You'll help?" said the bee.

"Yes."

"Oh, thank you, Miss Pickles! I'm just glad they didn't get you too. Were you out of town or something?"

"Yes."

"Well, lucky for you—and E. M., whoever that is," said the bee. "If you know this E. M., Miss Pickles, I hope you'll be telling him everything I told you. I don't know how long the creep's patience is going to hold out..."

"Yes."

"I hope E. M. understands the situation. I mean, if it was up to you and me, we'd quick give up the gold to save the lives of our loved ones. Am I right?"

"Yes."

"All the gold in the world is worthless if our loved ones aren't safe and sound. Am I right?"

"Yes."

The bee paused for a moment as if waiting for Little Pickles to say more. Then she said, "Well! I must get back. I promised Jumbo I'd audition the talent for tonight's talent show."

"Yes," said Little Pickles.

"It's been great talking to you, Miss Pickles. You're a very good listener."

"Yes."

Buzzzz. Flick-flack.

"Good-bye, Miss Pickles. I hope we can meet again sometime—under better circumstances, of course."

"Yes."

Then the door softly closed.

"Whew!" said Little Pickles.

"Aha!" cried Spider Kane, leaping out from behind the kitchen curtains. "Aha! Aha!" The spider laughed happily to himself as he limped around the room, clenching his fists and shaking his head.

"What is it, Mr. Kane?" cried Leon.

"That poor bee!" cried Little Pickles. "What in the world was she talking about?"

"What creep? What gold?" said Leon. "Did she mean the ants' gold?"

"Yes, I believe so, I believe so," said Spider Kane. Then he looked sharply at Leon. "Lieutenant, did you collect the blue notes and the postcard?"

"Yes, here they are," said Leon, handing them over.

"Ah, good! Thank you." The spider glanced at the postcard. "Yes!" he said with a broad smile. "Well, I must leave you now."

"Oh, no, please!" said Leon. "Don't go now! Tell us what's going on. We have to save Mimi

and my mother now or else that creep might—"
He was too upset to go on.

"Yes, please help us, Mr. Kane!" said Little
Pickles. And she started to weep again.

"Forgive me," Spider Kane said gently to
both of them. "But I'm afraid I need just a bit of
time to sort things out. Then later, I'll explain
everything."

"But this can't wait until later!" said Leon.

"What if this creep decides to do away
with all of them before nightfall?" cried Little
Pickles.

But Spider Kane pulled his gray cloak
around him. "Rest assured that our friends and
loved ones will not be done away with so soon.
Not as long as this 'creep' believes they are his
only link to the gold."

"What do they have to do with the ants'
gold?" said Leon.

Spider Kane held up one hand. "If you will
both come to my chambers tonight at seven, I
will give you a hot dinner. And *then* I'll serve up
some cold facts." Before Leon and Little Pickles

could protest, the spider saluted them and limped out of the cottage.

❧ TEN ❧

Promptly at seven o'clock Leon and Little Pickles arrived at Spider Kane's crumbling stone quarters.

"Come in," said the spider as he greeted them in his paisley dressing gown. "Let's go into the dining room and enjoy our meal."

"I'm afraid I don't have much of an appetite," said Little Pickles.

"Me neither," said Leon. "Can't you tell us what's going on first?"

"No, no, you must both take some nourishment before we attend to business matters. Come with me," said Spider Kane softly. And he led his two distraught lieutenants into his elegant dining room.

"Oh, my," said Little Pickles as she stared at the candlelit dinner waiting for them: pumpkin soup, a wild rose and nutmeat casserole with cranberry dressing, potato salad with chestnuts, poppy-seed cakes, and hot cinnamon rolls.

"Sit," said Spider Kane simply, and they did.

Throughout the meal none of them spoke, except to request a dish or offer thanks to the one who passed it. Leon was surprised to discover how hungry he actually was, for he had not eaten in two days.

Finally, when the last of the acorn-cap bowls had been cleared away and only the touch-me-not goblets filled with iced cocoa remained, Spider Kane pressed cherry-leaf tobacco into his pipe and said, "All right now, let's begin. First, I would like to share with you what I believe to be *the very key to the entire mystery.*" He reached into the pocket of his dressing gown and pulled out a postcard.

"That's the postcard you sent to the Hawk, isn't it?" said Leon. "What has that got to do with—"

Spider Kane held up a hand. "Wait, please.

Read it out loud, Lieutenant." He handed the card to Leon, then puffed on his pipe as Leon read:

"My dear Hawk,

I'm so glad to hear about your safe return—and your wonderful treasure. What a steal! Those ants are amazing, aren't they? Please tell Rosie, Little Pickles, Mimi, and Lieutenant Leafwing that as soon as I'm back from my trip, I'll be calling together our gang of six. After we celebrate your success, I'll outline our next little caper.

As ever,
E. M."

"Now," said Spider Kane. "Assume for a moment that *the creep* Ms. D'Bee spoke of has a very good reason to be interested in the goings-on in the Cottage Garden. Suppose the creep decides one of the best ways to get private information is to read the mail of other bugs, and he sneaks aboard the Garden mailboat. When he riffles through the mail, he comes across this postcard. What could he learn from it?"

"Well, perhaps that you were on a trip, and that you'd be back soon," said Little Pickles. "I should think that's about all."

"Think again, Miss Pickles," said Spider Kane. "First, the card allows our creep to study my handwriting. Second, it reveals my secret initials. Third, and most important, it provides him with the names of the members of the Order of the MOTH. Though in your case, Leon, the creep made a mistake. On the card I purposely refer to you as 'Lieutenant Leafwing' to celebrate your newly acquired title. The creep, however, must have assumed your mother was the lieutenant in your family. After all, you're quite young to be a lieutenant in any regular army."

"I told my mother that note was meant for me!" said Leon.

"And you were right," said Spider Kane. "Now, you may both wonder why this so-called creep would want to copy my handwriting. And why would he care about my secret initials? What does it matter who I name in the card?

The reason is that our creep misunderstands three little lines in this card. And his misunderstanding has been disastrous for us."

"What did he misunderstand?" said Leon.

"Wait," said Spider Kane. He picked up a newspaper clipping. "I'll get back to our creep and his misunderstanding in a moment. But first, Leon, permit me to explain to Miss Pickles the information I shared with you last night."

"What?" said Little Pickles.

"This is an article from last week's *Garden Times*. It is titled 'More Bad News for the Ants,' and it begins by telling us about the Harvester Ants of the Atacama Desert of Chile—"

"Oh, yes. I know about those wonderful ants," said Little Pickles. "They mine gold, then give most of it to the United Ant Charities to help needy ants. Rosie and I have done volunteer work for the UAC."

"I'm not surprised," said Spider Kane. "Perhaps you've heard then that the UAC's cargo ship was robbed on its way to the Ant Kingdom?"

"Oh, dear!" said Little Pickles.

"Yes," said Spider Kane. "And it seems that the sailor ant guarding the gold vanished also. It's believed he was drowned or taken hostage."

Little Pickles shook her head. "What is this world coming to?" she said sadly.

"I'm afraid I don't know," said Spider Kane. "Well, now, let's go back to our creep and his misunderstanding. Please allow me to turn back to my postcard and reread three lines." He picked up the card and read again:

> "My dear Hawk,
> I'm so glad to hear about your safe return—
> and your wonderful treasure. What a
> steal! Those ants are amazing, aren't
> they?..."

"Of course, those lines refer to the Moon Shadow Tapestry the Hawk acquired from the Tailor Ants of Borneo," said Spider Kane. "But what do you suppose our creep thought?"

"Oooh," breathed Leon. "He thought you were referring to the ants' stolen gold!"

"Precisely," said Spider Kane. "Therefore, I

believe our creep has no knowledge whatsoever of the Order of the MOTH. Instead, he was after a gang of gold thieves."

"Oh! Now I understand what Ms. D'Bee meant when she kept talking about that gold!" said Little Pickles.

"Amazing!" said Leon. "But who is this creep, Mr. Kane?"

"If my suspicions are correct, he is a creature who will stop at nothing to get what he wants," said Spider Kane softly. "He is a creature who will use all his talents and skills to manipulate others. He is a creature who is known in the underworld as the Bald Buzzer. But his real name is Raymond Johnson."

"Raymond Johnson?" said Leon.

"Yes. Raymond Johnson is a robber-fly," said Spider Kane. "And quite possibly the most wicked robber-fly on earth."

❧ ELEVEN ❧

Leon and Little Pickles stared at Spider Kane. "How—how do you know about this robberfly?" gasped Leon.

"I first heard about Raymond Johnson some time ago when I began performing in New Orleans," said Spider Kane. "Raymond Johnson was a legend on the Mississippi, for he had once been a fantastic entertainer. When he sang, he sang with total abandon. The music took over his whole body. Often, he couldn't keep from hurling himself about the stage—sometimes even into the audience. In fact, one night he tragically hurled himself right into a beach-party bonfire. He survived, but all the bristly hairs on his body were singed off."

"How awful," said Little Pickles.

"In spite of his accident, Raymond Johnson continued to perform. Bugs from miles around came to see him. He had a great talent for turning old-fashioned nursery songs into electrifying numbers."

"How original," said Little Pickles.

"Yes. The robber-fly had a great future ahead of him—until he got involved with the Hornet Underworld."

"The Hornet Underworld?" gasped Little Pickles.

"Yes. The hornets became great fans of his and gradually began to lure him into their criminal activities. It wasn't long before the talented robber-fly quit singing altogether and began hanging out full-time with the hornet thugs. His new cronies nicknamed him 'the Bald Buzzer'—due to his hairless condition, no doubt. And they convinced him to join them in acts of piracy along the river. Soon the Bald Buzzer became the toughest, meanest member of the gang."

"What did he do?" asked Leon.

"He attacked families sailing downriver—defenseless little bugs looking for a better way of life in the south. From all I heard, Raymond Johnson, or the Bald Buzzer, took a certain glee in stealing from these harmless creatures. Often he sank their tiny boats, leaving them stranded and penniless."

"Oh, how awful!" said Little Pickles angrily.

"Yes, it is awful," said Spider Kane. "And the waste of a tremendous talent."

"Well, what makes you think that the Bald Buzzer was after the ants' gold shipment?" said Leon.

"That conclusion was actually reached by the United Ant Charities," said Spider Kane. "Their investigators reported that Raymond Johnson and his gang of hornets were recently sighted in Santiago, Chile."

"Santiago, Chile?" said Leon.

"Yes, the ant port nearest the desert where the Harvester Ants' gold originated. Next, Johnson was spotted in the North Country where the gold was first delivered. And then more recently, he was seen near the Garden Creek. Therefore, the United Ant Charities suspects that Raymond Johnson was pursuing the gold all the way from Chile to the Cottage Garden."

"Oh, I see!" said Little Pickles. "But you

don't think he was the one who stole the gold?"

"No, I believe now that when he finally caught up with the ant cargo ship, he discovered that someone else had beaten him to it. He scoured the waterfront for clues, until my post-card threw his suspicions on our 'gang of six.' At that point he decided to capture all of you. So he sent out his blue notes and enlisted the help of Ms. D'Bee."

"Gracious!" said Little Pickles. "Everything makes sense now. Since the others can't seem to tell him where the gold is, he wants me to lead him to 'E. M.' and the gold!"

"Precisely," said Spider Kane.

"But who do you think really stole the gold?" asked Leon.

"That is the mystery we must solve later — when the Order of the MOTH is reunited," said Spider Kane. "In the meantime, our first concern must be rescuing our friends...before it is too late."

"Too late?" squeaked Leon.

"Yes," said Spider Kane. "You see, Raymond

Johnson will go to any lengths to get what he wants. He is brilliant, selfish, and totally ruthless."

"That—that means he might really hurt Mimi, Mom, and the others?" said Leon.

"Of course he will," whimpered Little Pickles. "And they don't even understand what he wants from them!"

"What can we do, Mr. Kane?" said Leon.

"All right. Let's suppose that Ms. D'Bee's creep is, in fact, Raymond Johnson, and that she is correct when she says that only he knows where the captives are. It seems obvious, then, that we must find Johnson before we can find our friends. And we must find him immediately. Tonight, in fact."

"Tonight?" said Leon.

"Yes," said Spider Kane, rising.

"But where will we find him?"

Spider Kane limped to his writing desk and took out his feather fountain pen. He quickly scribbled a note and handed it to Little Pickles.

The ladybug read the note out loud:

"Dear Mr. Johnson,
Meet me at Jumbo Nightcrawler's
tonight. I think I have something you
want.

Signed,
E. M."

"You must take this message to Ms. D'Bee at once," Spider Kane said to Little Pickles. "Tell her to deliver it to the creep she spoke of. Then meet Leon and me on the Bug Pier."

"What do we do then?" said Leon.

"We go into the club and wait for Mr. Raymond Johnson to show up. And then we will throw our net over him. Raymond Johnson has woven a web around the Order of the MOTH, and now it is our turn to weave *our* web around *him.*"

"But if he thinks we're bringing him the gold, won't he just kidnap us too?" said Little Pickles.

"Not if he can't identify us," said Spider Kane.

"But Saratoga can identify me," said Little Pickles. "I'm afraid she might be so frightened of him, she'll spill the beans."

"That is why you're going to wear a disguise," said Spider Kane. "And to be on the safe side, Leon and I will disguise ourselves also."

"How?" said Leon.

Without a word, Spider Kane limped to the old army footlocker at the end of his bed. He lifted the lid and began pulling out bits and pieces of costumes—wigs, berets, V-shaped beards, and several pairs of dark glasses. "Miss Pickles, can you play the drums?" he asked.

"No, but I've always wanted to."

"Good. Tonight you'll get your chance," said Spider Kane. "And when I introduce you in the talent show, your name will be Lady Jam."

"Gracious! You mean *we're* going to perform in the talent show at Jumbo Nightcrawler's?" said Little Pickles.

"Precisely. Leon, you play the piano, don't you?" said Spider Kane.

"A bit."

"Good. Your name will be Kid Ivory."

"Kid Ivory?" said the butterfly. "And—and who will you be?"

"Me?" Spider Kane put on a beret and dark glasses. He picked up his clarinet and tooted a jazzy string of notes. Then he lowered his horn and raised his eyebrows at Leon and Little Pickles. "In Paris and New Orleans," he whispered, "I'm known as Doctor Legs."

PART III

✎ TWELVE ✎

Thunderflies swarmed above the Garden Creek. As Leon and Spider Kane waited on the Bug Fishing Pier for Little Pickles, they heard the teeny flies whispering furiously, "Storm a-comin', storm a-comin'!"

Just as Leon was beginning to think that the ladybug would never show up, he heard the *flick-flack* of her wings. Then Little Pickles bumped down onto the pier, gasping for breath. "Mission accomplished!" she said.

"Yes, Miss Pickles?" said Spider Kane.

"What did Saratoga say?" asked Leon.

"Oh! She was so excited she started to shake," said Little Pickles. "She said that if E. M. turned over the gold, she was sure the creep would set everyone free, and that he would stop threatening her children. Then she rushed off to give him the note."

"Good work, Miss Pickles," said Spider Kane.

"Now, where's my disguise?" said the lady-bug. "You two look wonderful!"

Leon had to agree with her. When he'd looked in the mirror earlier, he'd hardly recognized the cool-looking butterfly in the dark shades staring back at him. He and Spider Kane were both wearing sunglasses, tuxedos, and tiny false goatees.

"How do I look?" said Little Pickles, pulling on a long wig.

"Let's hide your face a bit more, Lady Jam," said Spider Kane. He pulled a few strands of the red wig over her face. "There," he said. "Now, get ready, Bugland. Here comes the Doctor Legs Trio."

Thunder cracked the sky and a light rain was falling as Spider Kane, Leon, and Little Pickles entered Jumbo Nightcrawler's Supper Club. In the front hall they found Saratoga D'Bee and

Johnny St. Claire. Saratoga held a clipboard and pen. Beside her was a piece of slate that read:

TALENT SHOW TONIGHT—
eight o'clock till mid night

"Good evening, how are y'all tonight?" Saratoga said, smiling.

Leon thought the bee looked lovely in her apple-green evening dress with the matching cape. Her gold-key necklace dangled around her neck. She wore her rose-tinted glasses, and a tiny lilac bud was pinned to her blond wig.

"Very well, thank you," said Spider Kane. "Lady Jam, Kid Ivory, and I would like to enter your talent competition."

"Oh, yes?" Saratoga glanced at Spider Kane and Leon. But her gaze seemed to linger on Little Pickles. "Have I seen you perform somewhere before?" she asked the ladybug.

"I don't think so," said Little Pickles in a high voice. Then she coughed and turned her head away.

"I doubt you have seen any of us, madame," said Spider Kane quickly. "We have performed publicly only in New Orleans."

"Wait a minute...wait one minute!" said Johnny St. Claire. "I know this guy! I recognize that voice!"

Leon froze with fear.

"Who is he, Johnny?" said Saratoga D'Bee, staring intently at Spider Kane.

"He's Doctor Legs!" said Johnny. "The best clarinet player I've ever heard! I almost didn't recognize you with that beard, Doc!"

Spider Kane smiled. "You've seen me perform, Johnny?" he said.

"I'll say! My dad is Earl St. Claire. He used to play bass with you in New Orleans!"

"Good heavens," said Spider Kane, grinning. "I remember Earl. A fine musician."

"Thank you for saying that," said Johnny. "Tell me, are you performing here tonight?"

"If the good bee here will allow it," said Spider Kane, nodding at Saratoga D'Bee.

"Oh, you've gotta put these folks on the list, Saratoga!" said Johnny St. Claire. "Doctor Legs is dynamite."

"It sounds as if you're more than an amateur, Doctor Legs," said Saratoga D'Bee. "I'm afraid our local entertainment might not stand a chance in the competition."

"Don't include us in the competition," said Spider Kane. "We'd just like to try out some new material we've been working on."

"Well, all right," Saratoga said, smiling. "I enjoy good music as much as the next bug. Show them to a table, Johnny."

As Spider Kane started into the club, he leaned toward Saratoga D'Bee. "Excuse me, ma'am," he said. "But did you make that sign?"

"Yes," she said, puzzled.

"Well, it has a slight error. *Midnight* is one word."

"Oh, thank you," Saratoga said, and she corrected her mistake.

❧ THIRTEEN ❧

Inside the crowded club, the Woollybear Jugband was playing a toe-tapping tune. While one Woollybear swished the stiff bristles of her body against a washboard, the other blew into a jug.

Johnny St. Claire directed Leon, Spider Kane, and Little Pickles to a corner table near the stage. As he lit down on his chair, Leon looked about anxiously for the Bald Buzzer and his hornets. All the dancing bugs looked rather odd in their various outfits. They were wearing everything from dark turtlenecks to bright Hawaiian shirts. None, however, looked like he could be the wicked robber-fly.

"So tell me, Johnny," Spider Kane was saying. "How is your dad? I haven't seen Earl in a blue moon."

"I'm afraid Dad passed on a while ago," said Johnny, bowing his head.

"Oh, I'm very sorry to hear that," said Spider Kane. "Earl St. Claire was a remarkable bass player."

Johnny smiled and sighed. "Well, he certainly admired you, too, sir. I'd love to play music with you someday."

"Well, maybe you can sit in with us tonight, Johnny."

"Tonight? That would be terrific. What are you going to play?"

"Oh, I thought we might try something new," said Spider Kane. "Maybe a jazz arrangement of an old nursery song, like 'The Hokey-Pokey,' 'A Tisket, a Tasket,' or 'I'm a Little Teapot.'"

Leon quickly caught Little Pickles's eye. What did Spider Kane have up his sleeve? But Little Pickles only shook her head in bewilderment.

"Great," said Johnny. "You know, I heard an old song just this afternoon that had a nice melody. Now what is it called? Oh yes, 'Ducks on the Millpond.'"

Spider Kane stared at Johnny St. Claire with burning interest. "Ah, indeed," he said slowly, "that is a very good song."

"'Ducks on the Millpond'?" squeaked Leon.

"Just where did you happen to hear it, Mr. St. Claire?" said Spider Kane.

"Well, it's an odd story. When I was taking a walk, I heard it coming from the hill behind the club. It sounded like a moth singing. You know, that sort of dusty, resonant kind of voice moths have."

"I know it well," said Spider Kane.

"Anyway, the singing had stopped by the time I got over the hill," said Johnny.

"And there was no sign of the singer?"

"Nope. There was just this old bee house."

"Bee house?" Spider Kane sat forward in his chair. "Did you say 'bee house'?"

"Yes, a cement bee house, built long ago by mortar bees. But the singing couldn't have come from there."

"Why not?"

"Because the place is abandoned. The door was locked with a heavy padlock."

"Ah...Perhaps the singing came from a wandering gypsy moth, Johnny."

"Oh, yeah, I didn't think of that. Well, I better get back to work. If I can help you out onstage, let me know."

"Will do, Johnny," said Spider Kane.

As soon as Johnny St. Claire left them, Leon grabbed Spider Kane. "That's the Hawk in that bee house!" he said. "He sang 'Ducks on the Millpond' to the Tailor Ants of Borneo! That's how he got his tapestry!"

"Oh, my!" said Little Pickles.

"Yes, I know," said Spider Kane. "I imagine he was singing to the other captives, trying to lift their spirits."

"Well, why don't we go out there and find them?" cried Little Pickles.

But Spider Kane was now staring at the entrance of the club, where Saratoga D'Bee was greeting new arrivals. "In good time, in good time..." he murmured.

"But why wait?" said Leon.

"Because we must catch our enemy first," Spider Kane said. "And in order to do that, I want to try a little experiment."

"But, Mr. Kane," said Leon. "I think we should hurry out to the bee house! What if Raymond Johnson never arrives? What if we're just wasting precious time?"

Spider Kane turned to Leon. "I believe Raymond Johnson is already here, Lieutenant," he said softly.

Little Pickles gasped.

"Here? Where?" said Leon.

"Please be patient with me," said Spider Kane. "I am loath to reveal suspicions without proof. We'll just play our music...and see if it uncovers the beast."

A shiver went through Leon.

But just at that moment Jumbo Nightcrawler began shouting from the stage: "Ladies and gentlemen, please give me your attention!" The huge worm looked dazzling in the pink spotlight. Wearing a flowered silk vest and a black bow tie, he stared fondly at the crowd while he puffed on his fat cigar. "At this time I'd like to bring out a fellow who's never performed in public before. He's a little nervous. He's a little scared. So let's give him a big hand to make him feel welcome."

The bug audience started cheering and clapping enthusiastically. After a moment an odd figure stepped out from behind the curtain.

"Mr. Walter Dogtick, ladies and gentlemen!" shouted Jumbo. *Mr. Walter Dogtick!*"

"What in the world?" breathed Leon. He couldn't believe his eyes. Walter Dogtick was dressed in a very expensive-looking outfit. He wore a gold tuxedo and on his feet were four pairs of shiny black patent leather shoes.

As the audience applauded, Dogtick moved into the pink spotlight. "Hi, folks," he said shyly. "This morning I was feeling mighty blue. I was feeling so blue, in fact, that I decided to end it all in the Garden Creek."

The audience groaned sympathetically.

"But then by the creek, a miracle occurred that changed my whole life," said Dogtick. "And I decided to live."

The audience applauded Dogtick's decision.

"And now I'd like to sing a little song that describes what happened to me. I call it 'The Dogtick Blues.'"

Dogtick closed his eyes. He took a deep breath. Then he began singing in a slow, bluesy voice:

"My baby she left me one dark, foggy night.
My baby she left me one dark, foggy night.
She said, 'Mr. Dogtick,
You don't love me right.'

"I found a sailor ant a-cryin' near the creek.
I found a sailor ant a-cryin' near the creek.
He said, 'Take all my treasure.
Mercy's all I seek.'

"Gonna hire me a detective t' find my baby in
the fog.
Gonna hire me a detective t' find my baby in
the fog.
When detective finds my baby,
We're gonna live high on the hog."

The crowd cheered as Dogtick bowed again and again.

Spider Kane turned to Leon and Little Pickles with a look of utter amazement. "There's a lot going on here tonight," he said, "a lot going on…"

"Thank you, Mr. Dogtick," said Jumbo Nightcrawler. "You did an excellent job."

When the audience quieted down, Jumbo leaned toward the mike and said, "Now we have a really big treat for y'all. My friend Johnny St. Claire tells me that we're about to hear some of the best jazz music east of the Mississippi. Let's give a big welcome to the Doctor Legs Trio!"

"Come on, friends," said Spider Kane, standing. "Let's go weave our web." Then he started limping toward the stage with a bewildered Leon and Little Pickles hurrying after him.

✤ FOURTEEN ✤

Leon felt frantic as he sat down at the piano. He was desperately afraid Raymond Johnson was about to swoop down and grab the three of them.

But Spider Kane did not seem worried at all. "Key of F," he called to Leon. Then he lifted his clarinet to his lips and began a lively tune. Leon began plunking his piano, and Little Pickles tapped her drum.

Spider Kane's playing was astonishing. His high notes seemed to noodle about the air, then soar into the atmosphere. The audience went wild, screaming and cheering.

After a moment Spider Kane put down his

horn and sang in a deep, springy voice:

> *"Hello, Bugland,*
> *Call me Doctor Legs.*
> *I say, Hello there, Bugland,*
> *Call me Doctor Legs.*
> *I'm gonna get all you bugs*
> *Out dancing on the floor.*
> *I'm gonna leave all you bugs*
> *A-wantin' more 'n more.*
> *I say, Hello, Bugland,*
> *Call me Doctor Legs!"*

As Spider Kane went back to his clarinet, Leon studied the cheering crowd. Jumbo Nightcrawler and Johnny St. Claire seemed enthralled with the spider's performance. For once the worm's foul-smelling cigar had gone out. And Johnny St. Claire was wiping tears from his eyes.

Saratoga D'Bee, however, seemed completely unaware of the band as she greeted bugs at the door. Leon wondered if she was anxiously awaiting the arrival of Raymond Johnson.

Suddenly Leon nearly fainted with fear. A

hornet glided into the supper club. Then another. Then another and another. Saratoga D'Bee seemed oblivious of the hornets as she kept welcoming other new arrivals.

Meanwhile, the four grisly gang members glided to different parts of the room. One hovered near the ceiling. Another hung near the juice bar. Another settled at a back table, and the fourth loitered near the stage. Leon desperately looked about for Raymond Johnson. But he didn't see anyone he thought could possibly be the dreaded robber-fly.

When the song ended, the audience applauded wildly. With his eyes closed, Spider Kane mouthed, "Thank you, thank you."

Leon quickly flickered over to him and whispered, "Hornets are here!"

Spider Kane came to attention and scanned the room. "Ah..." he said as he spotted the hornet gang. Then he looked at Leon. "Now's the time," he said mysteriously.

Spider Kane turned back to the cheering crowd. "Thank you, thank you," he said above the roar. "It's so nice to play here tonight. At this time I'd like to ask a wonderful musician to sit in with us for a song or two. Let's have a big hand for Mr. Johnny St. Claire!"

"Yay!" the audience screamed.

Johnny grinned and buzzed forward.

"Welcome, Johnny," said Spider Kane.

Johnny saluted Spider Kane with his trumpet.

"And as a special treat, I'd like to add another member to our little musical family," said Spider Kane. "Perhaps if we give her a big round of applause, Ms. Saratoga D'Bee will join us up here too."

The audience clapped with enthusiasm, but Saratoga shook her head frantically. "No, thank you, I can't!" she called. "I have to meet someone soon."

"Oh, come on up, Ms. D'Bee," called Spider Kane. "Don't be bashful. We need you up here. Come give us a song."

But the bee kept shaking her head no. "I see our great singer is very shy," Spider Kane said to the crowd. "But if we all clap loudly enough, maybe we can convince her to join us."

The audience clapped and chanted, "D'Bee! D'Bee! D'Bee!" Leon felt angry and frustrated. Why was Spider Kane being so persistent in trying to get Saratoga to join them? Time was being wasted!

Saratoga still shook her head vigorously, until a couple of enthusiastic bog beetles scooped her up and began hustling her through the crowd. Spider Kane turned to the band and said, "'Hokey-Pokey'!" As the beetles delivered the bee to the stage, the band began a jazzy intro to the old nursery song.

Though the audience cheered madly, Saratoga D'Bee did not look at all happy. She straightened her blond wig and adjusted her rose-tinted glasses. As the band began playing a hot version of "The Hokey-Pokey," Spider Kane stepped in front of her and sang:

> *"Put your right wing in,*
> *Take your right wing out,*
> *Put your right wing in,*

And then you shake it all about.
You do the Hokey-Pokey
And you turn yourself around;
That's what it's all about."

Leon could tell Saratoga was fighting the urge to sing and dance. As Johnny St. Claire blasted away on his little trumpet, her head twitched in rhythm with the song. Then as Spider Kane started the second verse, Saratoga began softly singing with him in her deep, buzzy voice:

"Put your left wing in,
Take your left wing out,
Put your left wing in,
And then you shake it all about.
You do the Hokey-Pokey
And you turn yourself around…"

Suddenly Saratoga D'Bee threw back her head and screamed: "THAT'S WHAT IT'S ALL ABOUT!"

As the band kept playing, she seemed to lose her mind. She started spinning all over the stage. Then she picked up the mike and screamed:

"Do the Hokey-Pokey, folks!
Do it! Do it!
Put three legs in!
Take three legs out!
Put three legs in!
And shake them all about!
SHAKE IT! SHAKE IT!
SHAKE IT!
AHHHHH!"

Johnny St. Claire tooted away on his little trumpet. Leon banged the piano, Little Pickles pounded her drums, and Spider Kane blew his clarinet. As the band played, Saratoga D'Bee danced wildly around the stage. She buzzed forward. Then she zipped backward. All the time she was screaming and shaking. It was the strangest and most compelling performance Leon had ever seen.

"Flap those wings! Do the Hokey-Pokey!" she shrieked.

Leon looked at Spider Kane and noticed the spider staring with burning interest at Saratoga as she jerked her head from side to side and darted here and there. As she darted, her apple-green cape billowed out from her body, exposing two vibrating wings.

Leon was puzzled to see a big grin break out on Spider Kane's face. "Yes! Yes!" the spider exclaimed.

Then Saratoga screamed, "That's what it's all about!" and collapsed to the stage floor. The audience went crazy.

But Saratoga raised her head once more and screamed even louder, "That's what it's all about! That's what it's all about!" And she collapsed again.

The audience went insane with joy. Bugs were banging into the ceiling and turning flip-flops on the dance floor.

Saratoga raised her head once more, screamed, "THAT'S WHAT IT'S ALL ABOUT!", then collapsed for good.

Spider Kane took over. He began moving around the center of the stage, and as he moved, he played a scorching solo. His clarinet filled the room with wild, haunting sounds. One moment he sounded like a baby crying, then a rooster crowing, then a train whistling in the night.

The crowd screamed and applauded. Only Leon seemed to notice that while Spider Kane was playing, he was also pulling thread from the pocket of his tuxedo jacket. Cobweb thread!

Spider Kane danced around and around Saratoga, and as his hot-sounding music snaked through the room like a blue flame, he wove a nearly invisible web around her. By the time he finished his solo, his cobweb thread completely surrounded her.

Standing outside the sticky web, the spider lowered his horn, and staring at the bee, he began to sing:

> *"'Will you walk into my parlor?'*
> *Said the spider to the fly."*

Saratoga looked up, startled, and began rising from the floor.

> *"Is your true name Saratoga?*
> *Or is that a great big lie?"*

Saratoga buzzed toward the front of the stage. But she pulled back just before crashing into the web thread that separated her from Spider Kane.

"Is it really Raymond Johnson —
Here with your hornet crew?"

Saratoga D'Bee buzzed frantically to either side of the stage, but she found herself completely trapped. Spider Kane leaned toward her and sang:

"Well, it's E. M.'s pretty parlor, friend,
That you have stepped into."

"AHHHH!" Suddenly, in the middle of the stage, Saratoga D'Bee went berserk. She buzzed around in circles. Then she yanked off her rose-tinted glasses. She yanked off her blond wig. She was bald! She was a HE! And foaming at the mouth, he shrieked, "YES! YES! YES! I AM THE BALD BUZZER! THE GREATEST CREEP ON EARTH!" Everyone gasped, then began screaming. Even Leon screamed at the sight of the aging bald robber-fly with the huge bug eyes.

The Bald Buzzer rushed blindly toward Spider Kane. But since the spider was still on the outside of his web, the fly was instantly caught by the web's sticky strands and held prisoner. "Get him! Get that spider!" the Bald Buzzer screamed to his henchmen.

But the cowardly hornets all zipped out of the club, escaping the doom of their leader. As the Bald Buzzer screamed with rage, he became hopelessly entangled in Spider Kane's web.

The club broke into pandemonium.

"Call for the Waterfront Police!" Spider Kane shouted at a stunned Jumbo Nightcrawler. "Tell them you've captured Raymond Johnson!" Then he rushed over to Leon and Little Pickles. "Let's get out of here," he said. "Quick—before anyone discovers who we really are."

On their way out of the club, Spider Kane stopped in front of the imprisoned robber-fly. He reached through the web and yanked the gold-key necklace from around his neck. "Congratulations, Raymond," he said softly. "You've still got it in you. That was a splendid performance."

"AHHHHH!" the fly screamed.

Spider Kane gave him an elegant salute, then took off with Leon and Little Pickles rushing after him.

❧ FIFTEEN ❧

At the door of the club Spider Kane halted. "Wait!" he said to Leon and Little Pickles. "We have to help Dogtick!" And he led the way through the screaming crowd to the back of the club, where Walter Dogtick was cowering in his little outfit. The old tick was pressed against the wall, looking quite frightened and confused.

"Mr. Dogtick!" shouted Spider Kane. "Come with me!"

"Oh, no, please, don't kidnap me!" Dogtick cried.

"I'm not a kidnapper, Wally. I'm your old friend Spider Kane."

"Spider Kane, the detective?"

"Shhh!" said the spider, putting a hand over Dogtick's mouth. "Yes. Come with me and I'll take you out of here. Hold on to the back of my coat!"

"Oh, thank you, thank you," said Dogtick.

"Follow us!" said Spider Kane to Leon and Little Pickles. Then he led them all through the hysterical mob out into the stormy night.

Once they were outside, Spider Kane hurried through the rain with the group to a leaf awning behind the supper club. There, Leon and Little Pickles hung in the shadows so Dogtick would not recognize them.

"Now, Wally!" shouted Spider Kane above the din of the wind-driven rain. "We don't have much time. Tell me quickly—how did you afford this fancy outfit?"

"I told you in my song, Mr. Kane!" shouted Dogtick. "I came across a sailor ant hiding in a cove on the creek bank. He had a bag full of gold, and he just gave it to me!"

"And where do you suppose he got this bag of gold?"

"I don't know, he didn't say!"

"What *did* he say?"

"Well, he said something about being a traitor. Then he pushed the bag into my hands and took off, calling for a thunderbolt to strike him dead."

"Did that behavior not seem a little suspicious to you?"

"No—yes," said Dogtick, dropping his head. "I know I should have called the police or something, but I was desperate! I need money to hire a detective to find Pupa Leafwing."

"I have good news and bad news, Wally. The bad news first: Recently a United Ant Charities cargo ship was robbed of its gold shipment. Hearing your story, I've now concluded that the sailor ant guarding the gold was the thief himself! But once the deed was done, the ant began to feel great guilt and remorse, and he abandoned the gold to you on the bank of the creek. Therefore I'm afraid you will have to hand your gold over to the United Ant Charities."

Dogtick moaned with disappointment.

"But now the good news, sir," said Spider Kane. "As you know, I am a detective, and I am about to lead you to Mrs. Pupa Leafwing."

"What? What?" cried Dogtick.

"Yes! Come along!" said Spider Kane. Then with Leon and Little Pickles following, he helped Dogtick over the dark hill behind the supper club. As the four of them approached a thick clump of thistle, they heard the plaintive song of the Hawk coming through the storm:

> *"Ducks on the millpond, a-geese in the*
> *clover;*
> *A-fell in the millpond, a-wet all over."*

Spider Kane led the group through the high grass until they came upon the cement bee house built long ago by mortar bees.

"Now, Walter," the spider said in an urgent whisper, "this is what you must do. Take this key and unlock the padlock on that door. Then open the door and call for Mrs. Leafwing. When she comes out, grab her and rush her to safety. Others may come out with her, but ignore them. You must take Mrs. Leafwing away as quickly as possible."

"You mean *I'm* going to be the one to save her?" said Dogtick.

"Yes. And you can take *all* the credit, Wally."

"Oh, wow. Thank you. Thank you!"

"You're quite welcome. But you must promise me one thing, my friend."

"What?"

"That you will never reveal to her or anyone else that I am Doctor Legs—or that I helped you tonight."

"Why?"

"Because I must keep my various disguises secret for my detective work. Surely you understand."

"Ah, yes, sir. Yes, sir."

"Good. Now go and save your sweetheart, Wally," said Spider Kane, and he handed him the gold key.

As Dogtick stumbled toward the bee house, Spider Kane turned to Leon and Little Pickles. "Follow me," he said, and he quickly led them into the tall grass, where they hid.

As Dogtick struggled with the padlock, Leon could hear the Hawk's voice over the rain:

> *"Ducks on the millpond, a-geese in the*
> *clover,*

Jumped in the bed, and the bed turned
     over."

With great difficulty, Dogtick finally hauled open the heavy wooden door. "Pupa?" he called into the bee house.

"Yes?" came a tired, frightened voice.

"Come out, precious. I'm here to save you!" shouted Dogtick.

"Wally? Wally, is that you?" Then La Mère fluttered out of the bee house into Dogtick's arms. "Oh, Wally! You saved me!"

"Dat's right, precious."

As the two clung to each other in the storm, **Leon**'s eyes filled with tears. He was very glad that his mother and Dogtick had each other.

"Let's get outta here!" Dogtick shouted. "Come on, carry me, sweetheart!" He climbed onto La Mère's back, and the two of them took off into the storm, winging it away from the wild side.

"Come!" said Spider Kane. And he rushed with Leon and Little Pickles toward the bee house. As Rosie, the Hawk, and Mimi all stum-

bled out into the night, everyone grabbed everyone and shouted with joy:

"Rosie!"

"Leon!"

"Mimi!"

"Hawk!"

"Spy!"

"Little Pickles!"

"Thank heavens!"

"Thank goodness!"

"You saved us!"

"Let's go!"

❧ SIXTEEN ❧

The stormy weather had come to an end, and
dawn winds had scattered the clouds. Sunlight
streamed in through the windows as the latest
recording of the Hot Bugs of France filled the
Hawk's living room with jazzy swing music.

"No one suspected the theft of the ants' gold
was an inside job," Spider Kane was saying to

the group as he relit his pipe. "But as all ants are basically good at heart, the thief's conscience eventually got the best of him."

"But tell us, Spy," said Rosie. "How in the world did you ever suspect Saratoga D'Bee was really Raymond Johnson—the Bald Buzzer?"

"From the beginning I sensed something was not right about that bee," said Spider Kane. "But then three things in particular made me very suspicious."

"What?"

"The first was a misspelled word. On her sign for the talent show, Ms. D'Bee had incorrectly spelled the word *midnight* as two words. That's exactly how it was spelled on the blue notes you all received."

"Oh, I didn't even notice that," said Leon.

"What else, Spy?" said Rosie.

"Well, when Johnny St. Claire told us about the abandoned bee house, I realized not only that you were all being held prisoner there, but also that Ms. D'Bee had been lying to us."

"What do you mean?" said Leon.

"She told Miss Pickles she did not know where the captives were. But when Johnny mentioned the bee house, I remembered Saratoga's song, 'The Bee House Stomp'—in which she'd sung: 'Put them in the *bee house,* just for fun.'"

"Oh, yes! Of course!" said Leon.

"It seems Raymond Johnson's vanity about his clever songwriting got in the way of his better judgment," said the Hawk.

"Indeed," said Spider Kane. "The third thing that tipped me off about Saratoga was her gold-key necklace. Johnny mentioned a padlock being on the door. Most locks come with keys. And the nearest key at hand seemed to be the one dangling from Ms. D'Bee's gold chain."

"Oh, goodness," said Little Pickles. "I admired her necklace, but I never made that connection."

"But before I made my move against her, I needed absolute proof," said Spider Kane. "All this evidence did not prove that Ms. D'Bee actually *was* Raymond Johnson. It only indicated she was working more closely with him than she'd led us to believe. Therefore, to prove that the two were one and the same, I decided to entice the bee into performing for us."

"Why?" said Rosie.

"Well, in his singing days Raymond Johnson was known for his wild renditions of simple nursery tunes, such as 'A Tisket, a Tasket' or 'I'm a Little Teapot.' So when I began to suspect Ms. D'Bee might actually be Raymond Johnson, I decided to try an experiment. I thought that if I could persuade Ms. D'Bee to sing 'The Hokey-Pokey,' she might abandon herself and perform in Raymond Johnson's inimitable style."

"So that's what you were up to!" said Leon.

"Oh, Rosie, you wouldn't have believed how bizarre that performance was," said Little Pickles. "And yet how wonderful…"

"And then of course, the performance also disclosed a bit of scientific evidence that probably no one but myself would have gotten," said Spider Kane.

"What was that, Spy?" said Rosie.

"When Ms. D'Bee's cape billowed out from

her sides, I saw she had only a single pair of wings. Though bees look a great deal like robber-flies, bees have *four* wings whereas robber-flies have only two."

"Oh, that's why you cried, 'Yes!' when she was dancing," said Leon.

"Precisely," said Spider Kane.

"Wonderful job, Spy!" said the Hawk, and everyone clapped for Spider Kane's brilliant detective work.

"Now tell me this, Spy," said Rosie. "Why would Raymond Johnson disguise himself as a singing female bee in the first place?"

"I think the old boy was trying to kill two birds with one stone," said Spider Kane. "He disguised himself as a female bee singer first so he could scout the waterfront for clues to the missing gold without being recognized. But even more than that, I think he secretly longed to perform again."

"And the setup at Jumbo's allowed him to do just that," said Rosie.

"Exactly," said Spider Kane. "When Johnson

—disguised as Ms. D'Bee—told Miss Pickles he'd finally found his true home at Jumbo's, I believe he really meant it. In fact, I believe much of what he said to Miss Pickles was sincere. I'm afraid the poor fly was defeated only by the 'creep' within himself."

A hush fell over the room as the Order of the MOTH contemplated the tragedy of Raymond Johnson.

"What will become of him now, Spy?" said Rosie. "Years in Bug Prison, I suppose?"

"He deserves it, Rosie. But I would hate for such a tremendous talent to go to waste. I think, therefore, I'll talk to my good friend Judge Bagworm and see if a life sentence of community service might not be a better punishment for Raymond. Perhaps he could use his musical skills to inspire wayward youth."

"Here, here," said the Hawk, leading the group in a brief applause.

"Well!" said Spider Kane. "Our mission has come to an end. Though I'm afraid we'll receive no credit for it." The spider chuckled. "I imagine the United Ant Charities will declare Walter Dogtick Week to celebrate Walter's recovery of their gold. But don't let that discourage you, Leon and Miss Pickles. I'd like to thank you both for the splendid job you did throughout this entire mission. You were first-rate lieutenants."

As the group clapped for Leon and Little Pickles, the doorbell rang. "Ah, our pizzas have arrived," said the Hawk. "I hope everyone is hungry."

While the others headed for the kitchen, Mimi kissed Leon and whispered, "Hey, kiddo, would you like to dance?"

Leon smiled and nodded.

As the Hot Bugs of France played "Together Again," Mimi and Leon danced down the corridor of the Hawk's estate. They finally whirled to a stop in the Hawk's bedroom.

"I'm so glad to be with you again," whispered Mimi. "I missed you very much."

"You did?" said Leon.

"Oh, yes."

"I have to confess I was getting a little jealous. I thought you might be crazy about the Hawk by now," said Leon. "You two have been through quite a lot together."

"Oh, please," said Mimi, groaning.

"What's wrong?" Leon asked.

She quickly looked about, then whispered, "If I have to hear 'Ducks on the Millpond' one more time, I'll scream."

Leon laughed and whirled Mimi about the room. And when they finally came to a stop beneath the Moon Shadow Tapestry made by the Tailor Ants of Borneo, he kissed her.